Four Fathers

Ray French
James Nash
Tom Palmer
John Siddique

route

First Published by Route
PO Box 167, Pontefract, WF8 4WW
e-mail: books@route-online.com
web: www.route-online.com

ISBN: 1 901927 27 X

Editor:
Tom Palmer

Cover Design:
Andy Campbell
www.dreamingmethods.com

Support:
Ian Daley, Sally Fildes-Moss, Isabel Galan,
Roger Green, Sandra Hutchinson

Printed by Bookmarque, Croydon

A catalogue for this book is available from the British Library

Route is an imprint of ID Publishing
www.id-publishing.com

Thu book was possible thanks to support from
Arts Council England

Contents

Part One - Fathers

On the edge 7
Ray French

A photo of my father on Ilkley Moor 17
with his head missing
John Siddique

Model father 29
Tom Palmer

Exile, a memoir 37
James Nash

Part Two - Children

Aspiration 51
Tom Palmer

Letting go 71
Ray French

Inheritance 89
John Siddique

In loco parentis 101
James Nash

Part One

Fathers

On the edge

Ray French

After finishing a ten-hour shift at the factory my father would wolf down his dinner, rush outside, start chopping up wood, then hose down and scrub the back and the pavement outside our house. He'd disappear into his shed for a couple of hours next. Rattling and banging noises, interspersed with bursts of *The Wild Colonial Boy*, or a string of foul expletives would continue till my mother called him in for *News At Ten*, the only thing guaranteed to get him out of there.

Jayzus! The news! The news!

He'd come belting into the house, open the bottle of Guinness that he'd left warming in front of the fire and stir in a couple of teaspoons of sugar to take the edge off the bitter taste that stout always used to have outside Ireland. Then he'd sit back in his chair, mulled Guinness in hand, and have a good laugh at the newsreader, Reginald Bosanquet.

Would you look at that fella – he's a head on him like a bleddy turnip.

He couldn't relax till he was physically exhausted. He had been a stoker in the war and I often picture him down there in the bowels of the ship, frantically shovelling coal, keeping the engines running at all costs. He was just the man for producing endless energy.

He was born in Ireland, in a cottage on top of a cliff overlooking the sea – and he has remained a man on the edge ever since. He left in the late 1930s, driven to England by grinding poverty. After serving in the Royal Navy during the war, he lived for a while in the Channel Islands before settling in Newport, South Wales, a grimy industrial town just down the road from Cardiff. But in his head, where it mattered, he never left Ireland. To him, Newport was a place to be stoically endured, somewhere he happened to be stuck for fifty weeks a year in order to earn a living. But all the time he was looking forward to that two-week period in the summer when he could return to the auld country.

We lived in two different places, him and me. As a schoolboy in the late sixties I loved the hustle and bustle of the town centre, the promise of excitement that the crowded pavements and shops seemed to offer (but never fulfilled). But to my father it was hell on earth. I can only ever remember walking up town with him three or four times, to meet relatives off the train. As soon as we'd leave the house, he'd become anxious, irritable, and would walk at a pace I couldn't match. It was only when he'd stop every now and then to hawk noisily and spit into the gutter that I would manage to catch up with him. Eventually he would slow down a little. Once I drew level he would start to rant, staring straight ahead.

I'd fecking hate it up there in that town centre, so I would. I don't know how you could stand it.

It felt like a terrible judgement. If you actually *liked* that kind of thing, then there must be something seriously wrong with you, your values totally skewed.

Your feet would be worn out walking on that bleddy auld concrete, there's no give in it at all. Breathing in petrol fumes, bleddy teenagers walking past with transistor radios stuck to their ears, listening to a shower of fecking hairy gobshites screaming 'Yeah, yeah, yeah'. Jayzus, how could they call that music? It sounds like tomcats screeching. People coming at you from every direction, stuffing greasy auld chips into their faces, not looking where they're going, bleddy walking right bang into you, the ignorant cunts.

At the time I thought his hatred of crowds was just another sign of his crankiness, his obstinate determination to be different to all my friends' fathers, to draw attention to himself, and thus me, in order to make my life more miserable.

Now, looking back, I can see that it was panic. Back home, he could walk out of the front door, stride along the cliffs and roam for hours without seeing another soul. Something he often did, to escape the constant bickering and fighting. How he loved the smell of the sea in his nostrils, the feel of the salty breeze on his face, the sound of the curlews' cry.

Don't cross my bows, he'd mutter in disgust as another shopper cut across him, forcing him to slow down. His conversation was peppered with nautical terms. How he wished other people would keep a safe distance, just like ships at sea gave each other a wide berth.

He'd eye the crowded pavements uneasily, looking like he

11

was ready to run for it at any minute.

I came up here one Saturday night, years ago. Jayzus, never again, you'd be subjecting yourself to all kinds of indignity. Fellas roaring and shouting, staggering about mad with beer, you'd never know when one of them might go for you, or spew up all over your good clothes. The women are just as bad. Plastered in war paint, skirts on them no bigger than a bleddy handkerchief, shrieking and swearing at the top of their voices, completely out of control, no bit of shame at all. Oh Christ, don't talk to me about towns, there'd be no peace and contentment in a place like this. Oh Jayzus, just look at them, they're like fecking rats so they are.

He'd seen a documentary about rats – apparently if you kept on cramming more and more into a confined space, eventually they would attack and eat each other. This, he thought, was a warning for humanity and it was only a matter of time before London, New York or Peking erupted in an orgy of violence and cannibalism.

This kind of thing, of course, would never happen in Ireland, where a man had space to roam.

How I loathed the annual pilgrimage, that dreaded hadj – the hours of boredom on the desperately slow, packed-to-bursting boat train, followed by the hideous bouts of seasickness as we were tossed about on the foaming Irish Sea. Yet every year, when we came through the customs shed at Rosslare Harbour, white-faced, wobbly-legged, flecked with vomit, my mother's family would be there waiting to greet us (my father's were endlessly feuding and falling out, we'd go years without seeing them) with a loud cry of

'Welcome home!' I couldn't understand this – how could a place you only visited a couple of weeks every year be your home? One year, in an attempt to clear up this confusion, I told them I was Welsh and they laughed.

'Ah sure, what is a Welshman but an Irishman who can't swim?'

But then, even when we'd finally got to the place he'd been dreaming about for the whole year, my father couldn't relax. Back in those pre-Celtic Tiger days, Ireland was a Third World country, poverty-stricken and insular, a rain-lashed pimple on the very edge of Europe. Confidence was low and people were actively encouraged to blame themselves for the state of the country. In schools, teachers would regularly recite the homily, 'If the Dutch had Ireland they'd feed the world, if the Irish had Holland they'd sink it.'

My father would spend his holiday trying to mend the broken country he'd been forced to leave.

The relatives had barely finished inspecting their hand-me-downs before my father would jump to his feet, clap his hands and cry, 'Right lads, what needs doing?' He would spend the next two weeks digging, hammering, mixing cement, plastering and painting, convinced that Ireland was falling apart in his absence. No amount of pleading from his in-laws to for God's sake stop working himself into the ground, come inside and have a drink and enjoy his holiday could deter him from his frenzied activity. He would get up at six, come in when the rest of us were having breakfast two or three hours later and announce scornfully that he'd already repaired a fence, dug a ditch, or plastered a wall while the rest of us had been snoring in bed.

One year, woken by a cousin's snores, I got up at seven. I was making myself a cup of tea in the kitchen when my father ran past the window, pushing a wheelbarrow full of cement, singing *Nickety Nackety Noo Noo Noo*. He was a big fan of Ken Dodd's Diddymen and this, along with *The Wild Colonial Boy*, a rousing rebel song, were his two all-time favourites. He was delighted when he spotted me, and came inside.

If you're making tea I'll have some. I've a terrible thirst on me.

He congratulated me on my early rise, clearly taking this aberration for a change of heart. When he was younger, Dad looked a lot like the American actor Sterling Hayden, who was once described as 'a chiselled hunk of masculinity.' He leaned closer, obviously about to tell me something hugely important, something that was going to be just between me and him. His expression was disconcertingly similar to the character Hayden played in *Doctor Strangelove*, General Jack D Ripper. As his stare intensified, I was reminded of the scene where General Ripper tells Peter Sellers' RAF officer how the Commies have been secretly infiltrating our vital fluids.

His eyes grew large. There were tiny splashes of cement spattered across his face. He was breathing heavily.

They're a right bunch of fecking lazy bastards here in Ireland. There's not a soul about when I get up in the morning, still snottering and snoring in their bleddy beds. No wonder the country's in the state it is. If the Russians wanted to invade, all they'd have to do was land early

14

in the morning and the country would be overrun in a day.

But now, the eager glint in his eyes suggested, there were two of us to keep watch.

He slurped down his tea and asked if I wanted to help him lay a concrete path. Help him make the country a fit place for him to return to. I made my excuses and went back to bed, feeling horribly guilty, lacerated by the wounded look in his eyes. Here he was offering me one last chance to form a lasting bond and I had fled in alarm. A weedy only child, whose hero was the effete and melancholy Kinks singer, Ray Davies, I never figured out how to connect with him. I hated manual labour and, on the few occasions when we'd attempted DIY together, he'd flown into a rage at my incompetence after a few minutes and told me to feck off out of it. I always disappointed him and he always scared me, his rage and paranoia threatening to overwhelm me if I got too close. I preferred the guilt and pain of distance.

He's in his eighties now, still living in Newport, frail and white-haired, his manic energy diminished. Rarely leaving the house, no interest in the outside world. It used to drive me crazy, the way he would go on and on about how he was going to move back to Ireland, the needle stuck. These last few years he's stopped mentioning it.

Ah, it's not the same place now at all.

My mother goes back nearly every year still, but he stays in Newport and I come down to keep an eye on him while she's away. I'd give anything now to hear that auld blarney

15

about him going back to live in Ireland. Without that fantasy to sustain him he's slowly fading away.

When I come down to Wales with my own family now, my mother always accepts an invitation to come out with us for a spin in the car, a drink, a trip to Cardiff for the day. But it's almost impossible to prise Dad away from the house.

Ah no, you go. I wouldn't be interested in that kind of thing.

'Come on, it's a lovely day.'

I have this vision of him walking through the park with my daughter, smiling as he listens to her chatter.

'Just for an hour.'

He'll start to lose his temper.

I told you I don't want to go, are you deaf or what? Go on now if you're going.

My daughter begins to look uneasy. My mother has that pained look on her face. I drop it. We go without him. He stays at home on his own, reading the Irish newspapers that my mother's family still send every week.

There he sits in the gathering darkness, reluctant to turn on the light and waste electricity, shaking his head in bewilderment at what kind of a place the auld country has become, as strange and unwelcoming as Newport ever was.

A photo of my father on Ilkley Moor with his head missing

John Siddique

Before my father was mine, before he was headless through my mother's shaky use of the viewfinder, he was just Mohammed Siddique. Named, like so many after the Prophet, his surname meaning friend. His name showed him to be of middle class roots, a trading family, carpet merchants with a stall of bright rugs for sale. I haven't got that photo. I have been through all my albums and boxes where things like that live, I guess it must be at the back of Mum's drawer, where she stuffs things away. I have so few photos of either of them. My dad had a Polaroid camera. The film stock of the day has not survived that well. He drove a Morris Minor, black of course. This is when this story is set, when Morris Minors were black, before I was the first-born, before his car aspirations grew to a black-finned Zodiac, and before their solution to loneliness – marriage – turned my parents into who they were to become.

Mohammed Siddique rises at five thirty every morning. He goes out with just a towel round him and washes his body with cold water, shocking his teeth to a grin, in the whitewashed outhouse. Brown feet on the Yorkshire stone floor, his light palms stroking the water over the round of his shoulders. He uses the back of his hand to wet the middle of his back. He doesn't use the towel except to cover himself on his way back across the yard, he likes to drip-dry, squeegeeing his skin with his fingers. Back in his brown room he dresses ritually from the dark wardrobe. Through the nets, it's light already, he looks at the wet footprints across the lino. He puts on a white shirt, his socks and white Y-fronts, and chooses a tie. He has four suits, wears three on rotation, saves one for the weekend. It is Monday morning. Feeling a little gassy from the two bottles of Guinness he drank while watching television last night, he takes a couple of Moorlands indigestion tablets. Standing in the kitchen without trousers he makes chapattis to have with cold chickpea dhal and yoghurt for his breakfast. He'd taken a trip to Bradford on Saturday to buy flour, coriander and chillies. He'd shaken hands and talked in the language he'd talked in when he was a boy. He Brylcreems his hair. Short back and sides and quite long on top, most of the lads at work wear their hair like this. He enjoys his reflection as he works his comb through the shining blackness over and over, scraping his scalp, then cutting a line, high on the left with the end tooth of the comb, to make a white line parting. Perfect. As he pulls the door behind him, he hears Jack Thirsk opening the gates to his yard.

'Morning Jack.'

'Hello Siddique.' Everyone calls him Siddique. 'It's a fine one, isn't it?'

'It is. How are the horses?'

'Come and see for yourself,' Jack says, so my father goes into the yard behind him. Jack's a bit horsy himself, a long jawbone, gawkily handsome for all his twenty-six years. My father touches the cheek of one of the black horses. Its hot face presses into his hand as he runs his fingers in a tickle under and into the softness next to the bone.

'Off to work then lad? Dexine's, isn't it, where you work? I'd hate the smell in there.'

'You don't notice after a while,' my father says. 'I like the smell of the rubber. It sort of fills you up. Anyway it's a good firm, not like working in the mills where you're watched all the time.'

'I'd rather work for myself,' Jack says.

'I think about opening a little shop,' my father says. 'Maybe selling food and drink.'

'Aye, well it's not an easy game, food. Are you getting a sandwich for your lunch? I'll walk with you.'

The rest of the street is up and about behind their windows. They walk back past number six and go into the Polish shop. The woman there makes all the men their sandwiches every morning. My father gets two, one for lunch and one for morning break. The shop is cluttered and things are piled in strange combinations, lighter petrol and shampoo next to bread and glass jars of sauerkraut. He also gets twenty Park Drive, he's left his pipe on the sideboard. He always settles up with Mary – as everyone calls her, no one ever calls her Marzena – at the end of the week.

Jack lingers a while, being chatty and charming as she

21

makes him a breakfast sandwich, my father says goodbye to them both and heads off down Molesworth Street, dropping the plastic wrapping from the fags on the floor and pulling the smoke deep to feed himself on his walk up John Street, thinking about his girl Norah. They'd been out to the pictures on Friday night. He likes living on his own, but he's tired of being by himself. What's he supposed to do? He's thirty-two now. When was he going to settle down, have a family? God, he sounds like one of his father's letters. Norah and Siddique had been for a drink in the Dick Whittington after the film, they talked about the coming holidays. She's going home today to see her sister in Portadown; maybe he'll ask her when she gets back.

He walks past Lennon's supermarket and cuts across and along Yorkshire Street, walking the long way. He likes to browse Armours' camera shop window. Then he heads down to Cheetham Street and over to Spotland, where the bright blue of Dexine's gates and spiked railings rise proudly in the June morning, standing out from the smog-black brick of the houses lined up like rows of bad teeth along Spotland Road. Only the steps, ritually donkey-stoned clean, stand out from the repetitive faces of the house fronts. Even though it's sunny, it is cold in the shadow of the long sheds. He 'mornings' his way along the length of the works to the boiler room, where he has a crafty cig. You're not allowed to smoke anywhere on site. The boiler is big and red and beautiful, roaring noise and heat. He can't help rubbing his hands together by its glass face, then turning around and warming his arse. Peter is already in there. A year younger than my father, the same long-on-top hair, but mousey, he has a lived-in face. They work at neighbouring presses in the main shed. Outside the voices grow as everyone arrives for their shift, men of all shades, English, Hungarians, Indians and Poles.

Peter talks like a machine gun, filling all the spaces, his sentences overlapping, never allowing anyone too much room.

'It's The Wakes y'know. Looks like it's going to be hot again, last week was amazing. Town's going to be deserted with everyone away. You're allowed a holiday y'know.'

'I'm trying to save up,' my father says.

'I wish I was off somewhere,' Peter begins his next rattle, 'Why don't we take a run up to Blackpool this Saturday, meet some girls, eat some fish and chips, you've got a car.'

'Seeing someone this Saturday.'

'You old bugger, you've always got one on the go. Come on before we get the sack.'

They enter the main shed together. It's a noisy, thick-aired, but peaceful place. My father enjoys just getting on with things, as most of the men seem to, deep in their own heads, as meticulous as the parts they make. The shed is a vast black room with yellow pillars, piles of finished aircraft fittings everywhere. The rubber presses, all in a grey line, rise and fall and hiss slowly, water flowing through their arteries, moving the vast weights that shape the soft rubber. He goes to the

Barwell machine, where two boys are cutting the extruded rubber blanks into lumps that look like elephant dung. He smiles at this thought, but doesn't say anything, just a 'Good morning, how's it going? Thanks lads,' to the two blokes who run the machine, who stay bent over all the while catching the dungy pieces and loading them into shining black rows in bread trays. He takes two trays and goes back to the main shed. Peter is setting up his first run.

'What are you grinning for?' Peter says.

'Nothing much,' my father replies remembering the dusty town road of his childhood in Jalhandar. The timber man had a couple of elephants, and six-year old Mohammed would always rush out when they were coming past, dancing around in his lunghi. He would run his hand up the tree-like leg of the elephant and it would respond to him by touching his throat with the soft moving sparsely rough-haired, blowy warmth of the end of its trunk. The lovely lippy curve so gentle. He would giggle wildly, pulling his chin into his throat.

'Where's Stonehenge?' he asks.

'What?' says Peter.

'It was on telly last night.'

'I think it's in Somerset. Why do you want to know?'

'I just thought it looked like an interesting place, I'd like to go there and take some photos.'

'You're a funny one,' says Peter.

'I'm saving up for a Polaroid,' my father says. 'Put some money down on one, and I'm paying it off every week. Only seven weeks to go on it. I love taking pictures. Just imagine

24

being able to see the photo as soon as you've taken it.'

'It's a long way to Somerset,' says Peter.

'Pete?'

'Yeah.'

Father comes round his press and stands straight, letting his spine lengthen, he cricks his neck a bit.

'Could you just give me a hand stretching this out? Just hold it on the other side.' He is running two jobs at once as the presses take an age to descend and come up again, so they both draw the stretchy black sheet over the mould base of machine A7, which is all set up to make anti-shock mats for Ferrantis in Oldham. They work quietly together setting up and off-loading their presses, my father juggling between the two machines and Peter lending a hand with A7 when needed.

'You know I've got a girl?'

'What? The Irish one you were telling me about?' says Pete. 'You've been going with her a while haven't you? What about that other one?'

'Susan?' my father picks up. 'No, not going anywhere.'

'Nice though.'

'I like Norah,' says my father. 'I love her actually.'

'Christ fellah.'

'I wanted to ask you something. I've known you a couple of years now Peter. Would you be my best man?'

'You can't marry a white girl.'

'I haven't asked her yet, but I'm going to.'

'It's not right,' says Peter, 'It's alright, you taking them out

25

an' all, but its not on fellah. You're a good man, but you should stick to yer own. It's just wrong Siddique. Can you not get yourself an Indian girl, you have to get one of ours?'

'Never mind,' says my father. 'I'd be good to her you know, I do want her.'

He turns back to his own press. It's on the rise now, steam coming off the newly-made fittings, he squeezes his hand into the inch-wide gap that is full of heat. He's done this so many times now, he's learned not to burn himself on the slab's edge. He pulls each piece out keeping his eyes directly fixed on his job. He can feel Pete moving around his press, sorting the pressure setting for his run. He should be wearing gloves, but he likes to feel the rubber against his fingertips. He likes the way it rolls up and stretches, and comes out from the mould. He takes a batch to the trimming room, where the excess is cut off by teams of ladies wielding scissors as if they were extensions of their fingers. He's not supposed to leave his press, a girl will come and get his pieces, but he needs to go to the toilet, or at least that's his excuse to get out of the shed, and he might as well take these through.

'Save the girl a trip,' he says to the foreman.

He sighs as he pisses, manages to squeeze a bit out. He takes his time washing his hands. If he drags it out it'll be breakfast-break soon. They have a stop for a sandwich, then have a late lunch at Dexine's. It's just one of those things they've always done. It makes the afternoon go quicker.

'You're mad you know,' says Peter sidling up to my father in the tea queue. There is a vast mutter and rumble as

26

everyone comes in through the blue wooden door for their brews and butties.

'Just leave it Peter,' my father replies. 'I'll ask someone else.' He keeps his eyes fixed on the cup that the tea lady puts into his hand.

'Siddique, I'll do it, but you're really asking for trouble, you know. People in Rochdale don't like that sort of thing.'

'I don't really care what people think,' says my father.

'What about the girl? She'll get it in the neck too, you know.'

'I know,' my father says, not knowing.

'I'll do it,' says Peter again.

'Thanks, Pete. I knew I could ask you.'

'So what about Blackpool then?' Peter says. 'Let's just leave that be. Tell me when you've got a date for it.'

'I haven't even asked her yet, remember,' my father says.

They go over to one of the big tables with their tea and sandwiches; my father unwraps the brown paper bag, takes out his butty and ponders while he bites. His dark eyes take in the room, everyone in their white overalls. Seems strange to work in a place like this and have white overalls he thinks.

'We could always go the following weekend,' he says. 'We could go on the coach, that way I could have a drink.'

Before my mother and father were mine, they were Norah O'Neill and Mohammed Siddique. He was a handsome Indian man who liked taking photos. She was a girl who had seen a vision of the Virgin Mary during an air raid when she was eight years old. Both of them had moved to England in the late 1950s to find work, and to leave things behind. With the exception of their wedding album, I can't find any photos of them together.

Model father

Tom Palmer

When you enter Dubrovnik you realise you are in a special place. Adjusting your eyes from the scale of the mountains and the mass of water stretching beyond the horizon to Italy, you walk over a footbridge, under a stone portcullis and into the old town, always aware of the sea churning in the gulley beneath you.

A city with a history to match any other in old Europe, the first thing you see in Dubrovnik is a map of where Serbian shells hit a few years ago: a bird's eye view of the city dotted with asterisks and red triangles marking where paving stones exploded and seventeenth century buildings were burned out. And yet, this was not a place people fled from, but a place some of the country's displaced came to, escaping from the mountain borders between Croatia and Serbia. Thinking sober thoughts, you walk on the inside of the twenty-foot-thick city walls. Then round the corner to a wide high street made of footstep-polished stone. There is no sound of cars. Only footsteps echoing off palaces, cathedrals and monasteries clustered together on this outcrop of rock – and off the church that squats in the shadow of the cathedral.

It was in the church that I first saw the statue of St Blaise. Made of hammered silver, it reflects the dull light of the church in its dimples. Created by a local fifteenth-century metalworker, it was the only thing in the church to survive Dubrovnik's 1667 earthquake. A few inches high, the statue holds a tiny reproduction of the pre-earthquake city. In 1668 the architects of today's Dubrovnik kept strictly to the fine detail of St Blaise's model when rebuidling.

The statue and its model made me see my father as my father again, not a man dying, then dead.

In 1987 my parents travelled to Dubrovnik. I had seen their photographs of the walled town, the fleet of wooded islands in the deep blue water beyond it. I no longer have any of those photographs. Just memories of the photographs. But I knew that they had been to Dubrovnik. And I could imagine my father with his camera, my mother with her guide book, the pair of them breakfasting in the hotel, then wandering the alleyways of the old town until lunchtime.

Both in their second marriages, my parents brought up three children, two girls and, the youngest, me. Once I was old enough to be left at home, they began to travel to all the places they had only travelled to in books before. The books that directed their journeys were on a narrow wooden bookshelf just outside the bathroom door. *As I Walked Out One Midsummer Morning* took them to post-Franco Spain. *Crime and Punishment* to St Petersburg. Rebecca West's *Black Lamb and Grey Falcon* to Yugoslavia and Dubrovnik. They planned to go to China and Turkey and Morocco, but Dubrovnik was the last place they went. After they died

Yugoslavia collapsed.

I was in Dubrovnik to research my own book. The storyline about a young man who is trying to get over the death of his parents. It is set during the 1990s war in the Balkans. He has not learned to grieve his parents, so he grieves for the Bosnians instead, obsessing on details of the impact of war on individuals, finally going to the country with the absurd idea that he can help.

I wasn't clear how the story would end. Which is why, when I saw that model of Dubrovnik in the arms of St Blaise, I was so shocked.

During the war in the former Yugoslavia, more than two million people were displaced. We all saw the images from our sofas, feet up on coffee tables: a straggle of people coming up the hill towards us, squinting into the camera, a range of snow-cold mountains behind them. All of them with bags and suitcases and holdalls. Some in the backs of trucks or carts, their hands hiding their eyes. Some with mattresses, sofas and coffee tables on carts.

Sometimes a group of these people would get together in their new home (on the floor of a sports centre basketball court only fifty miles from their village, or as far away as Pakistan) to make a model of the Bosnian village they had left behind. *My husband made a model of our town to keep the memory alive*, she said. *A few men have made models in this camp. It takes a long time to build a town because it isn't easy to find the materials in Pakistan. But my husband was very determined. He looked*

33

and looked and finally we found some branches that we could cut to look like small trees, we must tend the model all the time because the green turns yellow. The inscription on the model reads: *These are our houses, on the land inhabited by our forefathers, we are going back there…*

The model is immaculate. Made of moulded plaster, matchsticks, cellophane, strips of plastic. If you squint you can imagine it is a real cluster of houses.

Sitting there, in the half-light of the church, looking at St Blaise and his miniature Dubrovnik, I felt like I had been struck over the head. This model of the pre-earthquake town in its glass case, the models of the Bosnian villages before they were burned out, were all signs to me. Signs that I should not be examining Bosnia and its war, that I should not be dwelling on the one thousand-year history of an old European sea port, but that I was being directed towards my own past. To memories of my father, a man who was driven by his hobbies. Not one hobby, like supporting a football team or plant-hunting in the world's mountain ranges, but many hobbies.

Every few months my father would be obsessed by a passion. A passion that would last until the next passion came along. A passion he would share with anyone who wanted to share it with him.

The darkroom he built in the cellar where we developed thousands of images.

The telescope he poked out of the attic window every

34

night one summer, the whole family staring at the surface of the moon.

The old printer's blocks he filled with our discarded toys and displayed around the house.

Fishing from a North Sea harbour, showing me how to cast my lead weight into the sea.

War gaming.

Peg doll making.

Fourth division Halifax Town, circa 1981.

Family birdwatching sessions in a hide at Fairburn Ings.

Intense preoccupations flashing into our lives for a season, then passing, leaving artefacts around the house that we vied for when he was dead.

And the other hobby: making models of imaginary small towns and villages.

It started with my train set – which was really his train set, a previous preoccupation. We decorated it with chicken wire and papier-mâché hillsides, dotted them with villages made of tiny pieces of wood. Then he left the urban blight of the train set and began making models of villages, with churches and town halls, using pieces of shaped wood he bought at a carpenter's yard. He displayed them around the house. They smelt of sawn wood. Sometimes he experimented with colour. And texture. Creating lawns with green-dyed sawdust and roads. Sometimes he built cloisters and cathedrals and walkways and walls falling and rising with the contours of his papier-mâché bases.

The memory struck me hard and I laughed. I laughed out

loud in the church in Dubrovnik. And I wondered if he had made a model of Dubrovnik. Or if there was a model somewhere of the part of Leeds I was brought up in, as it had been when I was five, six, seven, eight. And I wished I could see it. I wished I could look up to the altar and see a statue of my father holding a model of my childhood in his left hand.

Exile, a memoir

James Nash

My father's father was a bare-knuckle fighter during the last years of the nineteenth century, with a reputation for competing in illegal bouts up in the hills above his native Rhondda Valley. Some of my grandfather's violence spilled over into his domestic life and my father, a year underage, joined the army and left South Wales. It was the late twenties and he was shipped off to India as soon as he had finished his basic training. I can only guess at the journeys which my father made from the little pit village where he grew up. He boxed and played rugby during his time in the army. I have a whole series of team photographs of my brawny dad sitting among rows of other young men. His curly black hair is even then threaded with white and his grey eyes shine as silvery and pale as they did throughout my childhood. There is another photograph of him on a pony wearing a helmet and holding a polo mallet in his hand. The pony looks a bit depressed.

My father and mother travelled up and down the country during the war. Amongst the first to be called up, he spent most of his time training troops, with many tours of duty in the north of England. They did spend some time with his family, my granny widowed and now remarried. But my mother hated the shut-in feeling of the looming hills which sprang out of the back garden of their terraced house. Or perhaps it was my father who was more uncomfortable there, on his long-leave weekends. He had, after all, grown accustomed to wider horizons. After the war they bought a house and settled in West London, where my two brothers, my sister and I all grew up. My eldest brother found it unendurable and got married at nineteen.

I don't think my father ever left the army. It was imprinted on him like the tyre tread of a heavy military vehicle. I remember in particular two encounters with him, unusual because his interactions with his children were generally quite impersonal. He mostly dealt with us as a group, lined up as if we were a small, crack regiment he was inspecting. His demeanour was invariably formal, strict and terrifying. Were his hands behind his back? Did he have a swagger stick tucked under his arm? He had perfected a stare which seemed to penetrate any lie, or even the smallest straying from the truth. Minor infractions of behaviour prompted a volcanic display of temper.

The first encounter was short and brutal. I was washing up, in the desultory way of someone with other things on his mind. Aged about fifteen, I had been left a list of tasks to do, one of which was to mow the lawn in the back garden. To my horror I had run the mower over a stone and broken it. It lay in pieces on the garden path. I didn't know how I was going to tell him. He was upstairs asleep after driving to Wales and back in the same day. His sister had died and he had gone to the funeral. Mum was out shopping, my sister with friends, my brother at work. The next thing I knew I had been punched, low down in my back, with tremendous force. I fell forward over the sink, winded with the pain, my arms up past the elbows in soapy water. I turned, to find his hot breath on me, his face, inches from mine, still creased and heavy with sleep.

'You little bastard,' he said. 'What on earth did you think you were doing?'

My first thought, which I was too frightened to utter, was, I'm not a little bastard. I'm bigger than you.

If height is the main measure of size, I was bigger, being well over six foot, with my father an inch shorter. But even at fifty-five he had the bulk and muscle of a much younger man, of a heavyweight boxer. And there was something elemental and huge about his persona which dwarfed all around him. I stared at him. Those silvery-grey eyes again. I noticed the sleep in the corners of them. His bristly black eyebrows. His hair completely white. The evidence of a broken nose. Spittle in the corners of his working mouth. And, without thinking, I hit him. It was no real blow. Not a punch. I used my forearm to push him, and then to thump him across his barrel chest, spraying soapy water over his immaculate shirt front. He looked astonished, and rocked back a little on his stockinged feet. I braced myself for another blow. And then, with a wary almost frightened look, he left the room, shaking his head as I had seen fighters do when they had taken a hard punch. I was amazed, and leant back against the sink. Minutes later I saw him in the garden reassembling the mower. He never hit me again.

The second encounter was more complex. I was in my final term of school, revising for my A levels in my sanctum, the front sitting room. My Latin set texts lay open before me. Never had Tacitus seemed so dull and irrelevant. I was thinking about Steve – what would he be doing? Probably the same as me. He had started sitting next to me again in class, a month or so after I had been readmitted to school, bandages just visible below my shirt cuffs. Whispers of the scandal I had caused hung around the corridors for months, only going silent with my approach. Now he had started smiling at me again. And my parents were no longer looking at me with their eyes full of questions. I was listening to Nina Simone. It was 1967 and I felt myself to be almost ineffably cool. No-one else in the sixth form listened to this kind of music. Scattered around me were all the recent purchases from Collett's Jazz Record Shop in Charing Cross Road. I was not wearing my school uniform. My blazer was hung upstairs in my bedroom, together with the slim-fitting grey trousers that just passed the eagle eye of my form-master. I had on jeans, the grey, button-down shirt I had bought the previous week in Carnaby Street, the striped sleeves of which I concealed under my blazer, and grey suede shoes that tapered to a blunt point and had Cuban heels. I earned a lot of money at the local pub, bottling up the shelves, helping the cellar man, and taking the large dogs for walks. All my money went on clothes and records.

From outside I heard my father's car on the drive. The

dog started barking from the back of the house, and I heard my father's key in the door, and his deep voice calling out cheerily, 'Anyone at home?'

My mother's reply was muffled. She was in the kitchen, and I could hear the clatter of pans as she washed up after supper. There was a mutter of communication between them, the door opened and he suddenly appeared in the room, carrying two cups of tea. He seemed a little nervous. But sitting himself on the arm of the sofa, he put his tea down, handed me one, and loosened his regimental tie.

'How are you doing?' he asked.

I looked up at him. In the last year I had filled out. I had been training quite hard for the field events for school sports day; my particular strengths being in the discus and the shot. I felt strong and healthy. Whereas I could see a slight tremor in his hands, a slackening in his jaw-line, and a pink bald spot appearing on the back of his head. I was eighteen and he was approaching sixty. The contrast between us seemed enormous. It was impossible then for me to see the build and temperament we shared.

He inspected all the evidence of my working. The set books in German, Latin, French and English. The vocabulary lists. The notebooks. All neatly set out. These were all part of my escape route. Identity papers to enable me to take up residence in another city. He cleared his throat.

'See anything of that young Steve?' he said.

I jumped, my hands in my lap, apparently at ease. With the same attempt at self-control as when I was at the dentist, trying to hide my fear. I began to sweat a little. I looked at him. My father had medals for gallantry. But for him this was courage of a different order. There is a difference between bayoneting a straw figure and meeting the eye of the enemy you are about to kill. And this conversational opener went beyond any intimacy my father and I had ever shared. No training had prepared him for this.

'Yes, a bit,' I said.

'I don't know what he was playing at,' my father said. 'It was like he was stringing you along. If I'd been him, I'd have just thumped you. That would have sorted you out.'

Together we pondered the efficacy of the punch which sorted you out.

'We had some chaps in the regiment who didn't quite fit in. And they weren't big, well-set blokes like you. They always seemed to be shaving. Bit too smart, if you know what I mean.'

I did know. My face burned. By this, my father's informal yardstick of sexuality, about seventy-five per cent of the young male population of Great Britain in the late 1960s were homosexual. The remaining twenty-five per cent just couldn't afford to be.

'Your mother and I are a bit worried about you.'

I thought of the hours I had spent sitting on the edge of my bed, hearing my mother's tears, and my father's raging in a downstairs room, and smiled internally at this understatement. Some of the smile must have shown on the outside, because my father frowned. I quailed a little. But he

44

persisted in his new diplomatic approach.

'You'll be going off to university soon, and you can put all this behind you. I just need to ask you a question, Son.' His voice rose at the end of the sentence as if he was asking permission. My hands tightened in my lap.

'Your mother and I know that you earn a lot of money doing your job at the pub. You worked last summer during the school holidays. But you never seem to have any money. You never seem to save.'

For my father saving had an almost religious obligation to it. Never believing in hire purchase, he always paid in cash for everything. I think even having a mortgage was mortifying for him. Living on tick. He reserved his greatest scorn for people who did this. It was inconceivable that one could survive, breathe even, without saving. I didn't save. And he wanted to know where the cash was going. He was worried. I could see that. And it was more than the worry of a man overseeing the fiscal affairs of his family. But I couldn't see why. He probably had no idea how much I was spending. He didn't see the books, clothes and records I smuggled into the house.

Again the frown, but this time because he was thinking what to say.

'You're not being blackmailed are you, Son?'

My face must have registered the shock. He faltered a little, but still continued.

'You hear such things, stuff in the newspaper.'

I saw his fears clearly on his face. My money disappeared

without any signs of where it was going. I was vulnerable. I was being blackmailed. It was the basis of many scandals in the fifties and sixties.

I looked down at my lap. My father's presumption that I was caught up in a homosexual lifestyle, and his care for me in and through that, was startling. But most of all it was embarrassing. Having spent my adolescence keeping my privacy intact from my parents, my father had breeched it with one surprise attack and left me breathless. On the ropes.

I looked at him. His boxer's good looks, Spencer Tracy crossed with Victor Mature. Close to, the stray hairs, on his nose and ear-lobes were out in force. His eyes were full of a shocking kindness and understanding. He ruffled my hair. My eyes filled with tears. I had not cried before. Not once. Not when the doctors, one working on each wrist, stitched up my wounds, under local anaesthetic, as I lay in the operating theatre like a horizontal crucifixion. Not when the nurses, stiff with righteous disapproval and hospital starch, helped me on with my shirt. Not when, later in the same week, I had been asked to leave the school. Not when Steve stopped speaking to me.

I shook my head. And again.

'No,' I said, my throat blurred and aching with a kind of internal weeping. 'Don't worry. I'm not in any trouble. Nothing bad is happening to me.'

He looked at me. And I understood how he had been able to lead men. I had thought it must have been entirely by fear. Fear of his anger. His unquestionable authority. But he had also possessed this terrifyingly human understanding. Understanding without criticism. He grinned.

'Well that's OK, then.'

He sprang to his feet like a much younger man, and bellowed through the door. 'Now then Mrs Nash. How about some biscuits out here?'

When Mum appeared at the door a barely perceptible sign passed between them. And she visibly relaxed. My father uncharacteristically put his arm round her, and squeezed her plump shoulders.

'Come here, Vessey,' he said. Her maiden name. 'I love every acre of you.'

And the three of us sat there in the front sitting room, with tea and biscuits, until my brother and my sister came home.

Part Two

Children

Aspiration

Tom Palmer

I

Sam and Libby had been told they would never have children. There was something wrong with him. And there was something wrong with her.

'It would be a miracle,' the consultant said to end their final consultation at Bradford General Infirmary.

When they were told it would never happen, Sam phoned friends and family, one after the other, for three hours. He handled it calmly, delivering the news in a matter-of-fact tone, using up all his adrenalin to get the words out.

The next day the doorbell rang and Sam received a delivery of two bunches of flowers from Interflora. The flowers broke him in two. He could not speak to the man delivering them, nor listen to the advice about caring for cut flowers so they would not die too quickly. He nodded, held his hand up in apology, then closed the door.

The clocks had just gone back. The days were short and cold.

A week after the flowers, the overflow pipe under the bath came loose and water poured through the ceiling, bringing down a wall of loose plaster over the cooker.

'I can't cope with this,' Sam said, sitting down on the kitchen floor.

'I'll sort it,' Libby said quickly. After the delivery of the flowers she had taken over everything like that.

'Now we have to get some plasterer in to sort it out. Look at this wall.'

'I'll sort it,' Libby said again. She didn't mind about the wall. It was just a wall. She found a number in Yellow Pages and called.

Libby put her hand over the mouthpiece. 'He says next Thursday.'

Sam looked in his diary. 'I'll be out,' he said, having already decided that he would not be in the day the plasterer came. He hated workmen. Rather, he hated it when workmen were in the house, dreading being seen just sitting and doing nothing while a real man did his work.

'He says two hundred pounds,' Libby said.

Sam grimaced. He'd pay it if he didn't need to meet the plasterer. He'd pay anything so long as the plastering was done and he didn't have to look at the hole in his wall.

'This is a lovely big house,' the plasterer said.

Sam had come home to find the plasterer still working. Libby had invited him to join them for tea.

'Thank you,' Libby said, laying her knife down on the side of her plate.

Sam began to relax. The plasterer had said something that had made Libby feel good. Why should he feel guarded about that? He should feel good that Libby felt good.

'So? Do you have kids?' the plasterer said. 'Are you going to have any? Lots of bedrooms. How many? Three?'

'Four rooms,' said Sam. 'No kids.'

'No kids?' The plasterer held his hand over his mouth. 'You've got to have at least one.'

The no kids silence followed.

'It's not that easy for some people,' Libby said.

Once she had spoken she knew she sounded snotty. Every time the topic of children came up she tried to speak kindly, so that the person who said it would not feel bad.

'Oh, I know, I know,' the plasterer said. 'I'm sorry. Me and the wife. It was the same for us. We were told we had a two per cent chance.'

'I'm sorry,' Libby said.

'Don't be,' the plasterer said. 'I'll tell you the story. It was funny. Well, odd. Not funny. After we'd been told 'two per cent', we sort of gave up. We looked at IVF and all that, but we just couldn't afford it. Four grand! Anyway, I was out on this walk. On the tops. Just me. Thinking about stuff. I walk a lot. I was going along. I felt this hand behind me. Pushing me. No-one there. Like a really strong wind. But it wasn't windy. And it was a warm feeling. And I suddenly felt that everything was going to be alright. With the wife, you know? I don't know what it was. God or my Gran? I really don't know. But something was telling me. Do you know what I mean?'

Sam and Libby listened without speaking.

'And two weeks later,' the plasterer said. 'Bang. The wife tells me she's pregnant. Don't get me wrong. I'm not religious or anything. Well, I believe there's a god. But I think someone up there was telling me. Or helping me.'

The plasterer went back to his meal.

Libby could see Sam's eyes were full of tears. He normally filled uncomfortable silences.

The three of them sat round the table listening to the sound of the washing machine pulsing in the cellar below.

II

The Halifax consultant was huge. Six and a half feet tall, his arms and shoulders like a bull's. He met Libby and Sam without changing his stride, rushing them down a corridor.

Sam remembered the consultant in Bradford, he had examined Libby with a mechanical coldness and without a word; then stood in the corridor, backward-glancing them when they were taken to a room to be told by a junior doctor that they would never have children.

Sam was determined not to let Libby be treated like that again.

But the first thing the Halifax consultant did was make Libby laugh, really laugh. Sam tried to remember the last time he heard Libby laugh.

The consultant said he had seen Libby's scans from Bradford. And he was aware of Sam's prognosis. Then he said there was a form of IVF that could be an option. Something he'd like to try.

'At Bradford they told us IVF wouldn't work,' Sam said.

'But you're here?'

'True,' Sam said. Libby had wanted a second opinion. A second hospital.

The consultant nodded. 'Sam. Who did you see at Bradford?'

'Mr Robinson.'

'Ahh,' he said, raising his eyebrows.

Sam said nothing. Libby said nothing. Under the table their

knees angled outwards. Touching.

'I won't pretend that you're not a challenge,' the consultant said to Libby. 'Your endometriosis is advanced. Your cysts are huge. I can't imagine the pain you are in. I can help with that too. And Sam. We've got to get at your sperm. See if they're okay. We can do that. On paper, children look a serious challenge, yes. But,' he put his hands on the table, looking at Libby, 'you are a fertile woman. A very fertile young woman. Even with all that going on, I can see healthy tissue. Lots of healthy tissue. The lining of your womb. It's beautiful. You're going to be my star patient.'

Libby grinned and looked down. Her knee pressing against Sam's firmly now.

III

The testicle specialist needed to examine Sam to see why there was no sperm in his semen. He asked Sam to lie down on a raised bed in his office, rolling out a wide sheet of absorbent paper for him.

Sam felt like vomiting as he let his body fall back, his bare legs cold, his testicles dangling and brushing the rough paper.

This man was going to check the tubes that should be delivering the sperm. This man was going to handle Sam's balls. He remembered having his testicles felt like this before and the uncomprehending look on the doctor's face when he squirmed and resisted, as if the doctor was merely examining his hand or his foot. He could feel sweat accumulating in the small of his back, dripping down onto the absorbent paper.

When the testicle specialist's hands came towards him, Sam jerked away.

'Relax,' the testicle specialist said, his hands now rubbing the sides of Sam's balls, looking for the tubes.

Sam was sweating more, his legs, his back, his face, his arms. The paper beneath him was soaked.

'You must relax,' the testicle specialist said, exasperated, his hands withdrawn. 'If you don't relax I can't find the tubes.'

'I can't,' Sam said.

In the consultation room the testicle specialist said that he would have to carry out an aspiration, under a general anaesthetic. The operation would cost another £700 and Sam agreed, nodding enthusiastically to Libby.

The testicle specialist explained aspiration.

To acquire sperm they would have to open Sam's testicle sac enough to lift out one of his testicles, place it on the operating table and cut a small piece from it. That would provide the sperm needed to fertilise Libby's eggs.

IV

'Just do it,' Libby said.

'Okay,' Sam looked again at the plastic gun, moving it closer to her thigh.

'No. Stop. Stop. Not yet.'

To prepare, Sam sat at Libby's dressing table and broke open four tiny vials, pressing them hard against the table top before he heard them snap. Three vials contained powder, one water. He used a syringe needle to stir the powders into the water. He drew the solution back into the syringe. He checked it and double-checked it for bubbles, thinking he might kill Libby with a bubble of air to the vein. He screwed the syringe into the plastic gun and tried to be quiet clicking its recoil back. Then he turned towards Libby.

He had practiced firing the gun into an orange. But Libby was not an orange. Libby was his wife. And now he had to stick a needle in her thigh. He loved her thighs. He had watched her thighs as she had dressed and undressed before him. He had run his hands gently up and down her thighs. He had felt the inside of her thighs against the outside of his thighs as they made love.

'Do it now,' Libby said, looking away. 'And tell me a nice story.'

Sam told her about the hotel they stayed in on their honeymoon. A former palace on the banks of Lake Como. He described the view across the lake from their top floor balcony, three rows of mountains rising into the clouds, the steamers criss-crossing the water, leaving ripples like flies skimming the surface. He placed the gun against her leg. He reminded her of the pool behind the hotel. The trees and vines hanging over the water. The waiters bringing cappuccino and freshly squeezed juices to the poolside. He fired the gun. Libby jerked. Sam held the needle deep in her leg. He counted. One. Two. Three. Four. He told her about the eagle that soared over the lake outside the hotel one morning at 5am when they had both woken. Libby's eyes said, Take it out. Sam stared back at her with a deadpan face. Five. Six. Seven. He told her about the bottle of chilled white wine they'd had delivered in a silver bucket to their restaurant table every night, wrapped in a white napkin before it was poured by the waiter. Eight. Nine. Ten. He withdrew the gun. And together they watched blood rise to form a red bead through the pinprick hole in Libby's thigh.

V

Sam had on a pair of plastic socks over his shoes.

The operating theatre was smaller than the box room at home. The walls were hung with tubes and wires and dials, a hatch at the far end into a laboratory. Two doctors stood over Libby, Sam at her head. Libby's hand was attached to a large syringe, feeding a cocktail of pain killers into her bloodstream. Her legs were spread, feet up in cold metal stirrups. She was breathing deep and fast, her head moving from side to side.

'I think she needs more pain killers,' Sam said quietly, eyeing the syringe.

The doctor monitoring the syringe shook his head. He didn't think she should be in so much pain. This was only an egg harvesting.

Sam said nothing more. He didn't want to push it, didn't want to alarm Libby.

On the screen above the bed a thin tube probed around a grey cavity, edging towards small dark patches.

'There's another,' said a woman on the other side of the hatch. 'Twelve.'

'Twelve,' Sam said to Libby. 'Twelve.'

Libby tried to smile, but her face was set hard against the pain.

Sam took heart that she had not moaned for a few seconds.

'Is it okay now?' he said. 'The pain?'

Libby exhaled and started to cry.

'Thirteen. Fourteen.'

Sam sat at the end of the bed, stupid and helpless. Trying not to think that this was a torture chamber. The plasterer came into his mind unprompted. Then disappeared. Sam smiled.

'Tell me something,' Libby said, looking up at him. 'Please tell me something. Like before.'

'The desert?' Sam said, panicking. Where they had met.

'Just tell me.'

Sam described hard dry salty sand cracking like ice beneath their feet. Shadows stretching for hundreds of yards, the sun playing impossible tricks with the light.

'Fifteen.'

He described the nights. So little light that, casting the beam of their torch about, they felt they were on the bottom of the sea.

'Sixteen. Seventeen.'

'Seventeen,' Sam said. 'They said anything over fifteen would be good.'

'The desert,' Libby shouted.

The lone footprint of a gazelle. And their excitement, as if they'd seen a herd of a thousand gazelles.

'Eighteen.'

The way shooting stars would cut a hundred and eighty degrees of black hemisphere of sky in two. And the night they went to a sand dune, away from the rest of the party, for their first kiss.

But Libby was not listening. She was sobbing.

'Nineteen.'

'Stop,' Sam said.

The doctors looked at each other.

A glance.

A nod.

'Okay,' the doctor with the suction tube said.

'Okay,' the woman behind the screen said. And she disappeared with nineteen of Libby's eggs, into the over-lit laboratory behind the screen.

As Libby slept off the operation and the pain killers, Sam knew that they were injecting his sperm into her eggs. If the IVF worked, he thought, this is the moment of conception.

He took Libby's hand.

VI

'Call at lunchtime on Wednesday,' Debbie at the clinic had told them.

'What time during lunchtime?'

'One?'

At quarter to one Libby and Sam had nothing to say to each other. The day had gone okay until then. They had been buoyant. Excited. Anything was possible. But for the last fifteen minutes they had sat watching the clock, watching the phone, watching each other.

Sam volunteered to make the call.

Libby was pleased. 'I couldn't have done it,' she said.

But at five to one Sam was in tears. He was shaking. 'I can't do it,' he said. 'I can't speak. I won't be able to speak.'

Libby took the phone and smiled at him. 'I'll do it,' she said.

They both put their ears to the phone.

'Assisted Conception Unit.' Debbie's voice.

'Hello. It's Libby. And Sam.'

'Hello love,' Debbie said.

Sam tried to read her voice. The cadence of her vowels. It was a no. He could tell.

'I'm sorry,' Debbie said. 'The results were negative.'

There was nothing to say. Neither Libby nor Sam cried. Not immediately.

VII

The dining room was spotless, illuminated by side lights and a single giant candle. Outside they could see the light dwindling low in the sky over the hills to the west. A cloud of mist floated across the garden. Sam saw it, then a pair of ducks hurtling over the trees. He looked around the room.

A table set for six, an extra leaf in place to accommodate champagne glasses and two dish heaters, each with three tea lights flickering under metal grills. The room was wood panelled to waist height. There was a picture rail.

Libby's mum placed a large pot onto one of the dish heaters. When she took the lid off, Sam watched steam pour upwards like air from an underwater vent.

'Before we go on,' Libby's father said standing, waiting until all eyes were on him and for his wife to sit down. 'A toast.'

Libby was the first to put her fingers round the stem of her glass, catching her father's eye, smiling at him. He smiled back.

'To the new baby,' he said. 'In advance of its coming. God knows what it'll make of us all, but we look forward to meeting it.'

Sam watched the glasses chinking over the table, then Libby, who was smiling at her brother's wife, Jessica, heavily pregnant.

'Let's eat,' Libby's mum said, offering serving spoons to Sam and Jessica.

Sam began asking questions.

What kind of birth were they going for? Did they know the sex? Had they thought of names? Would they be staying in or moving out of London? A salvo that demanded the full attention of the happy couple and the future grandparents.

Until Sam ran out of questions.

'When are you going to have children, Libby?'

Jessica had asked the question.

Libby's mum filled the silence quickly. 'Soon, we hope. Don't we love.'

'Yeah,' Libby said, none of the finely-tuned phrases she had practiced for a situation like this coming to mind. Just a blank exhaustion.

'So what are you working on now?' Sam said to Libby's brother, David.

'Just the usual, really, Sam. Several accounts. I did a bit of work for the FA recently. That was interesting.'

But Sam wasn't listening. He was trying to work out whether Libby had said yes to Jessica to deflect the question – or if she'd changed her mind, decided they *should* try again. In the car on the way to her parents she'd said no.

'Yeah?' Sam said to her brother.

Libby's father filled Libby's glass and went to fill others, but saw they were all still full.

'I hope you do,' Jessica said. 'Have children, I mean. I think it'd be lovely to come here and have our children play. In the garden. On the moor.'

'That sounds great,' Sam said, trying to stop the thread of the conversation, thinking desperately where he could take it. But the idea of his child running around after David and Jessica's appealed to him and reminded him of his siblings, his cousins, large family gatherings.

This is what is at stake, he thought.

He looked over at Libby. She gazed back at him.

Letting go

Ray French

A sticky summer's day in London, my daughter and I are swapping the narrow, traffic-choked streets of grimy Walthamstow for somewhere greener and quieter. She is three, I am working part-time, and take care of her two days a week. We are on the North London line, which meanders lazily across the top half of the capital from North Woolwich in the east to Kew in the west. She stands on my legs to see better out of the window, and I hold her around the waist to steady her against the pitch and roll of the train as we trundle and clank past embankments, cuttings and gardens. I love this route – sometimes I glimpse an old man pottering in his allotment, or a church spire through the trees, and imagine we're somewhere deep in the country. I point out things I think will interest her.

'Look, they've got a swing in their garden.'

She presses her hands to the window to see. Then it's her turn to notice something.

'They've got a paddling pool.'

'Oh yeah. Do you think a little girl lives there?'

'Yes.'

'I wonder what her name is?'

She looks at me and smiles.

'Rosie.'

There are lots of girls called Rosie in her picture books. We establish that Rosie has a pony, and doesn't go to nursery two mornings a week like her, that her mam and dad take care of her all the time. Which, of course, is what she'd like. I dutifully list the benefits of attending nursery while she scowls, unconvinced.

Then it's my turn once more to find something of interest and make a story out of it, and soon the nursery issue is forgotten. When we are completely absorbed in a game like this I feel carried along on a current. Time is suspended, everything clicks into place effortlessly and things feel just right between us. Psychologists, naturally, have a name for this. It's called 'flow' – doing something enjoyable for its own sake, the opposite of the soul-crushing routine of other, working mornings. Three or four days a week I squeeze into a stifling, tightly-packed metal container to be thrust at high speed through a labyrinth of dark, crumbling tunnels into central London. Prolonged use of The Underground gradually chips away at your humanity – misery and frustration are etched into your fellow passengers' faces as deeply as tribal marks. Crushed between strangers, swaying from a strap dangling from the ceiling, I sometimes think, *Is this really my life?*

However if the tube is designed to oil the wheels of commerce, the North London line is perfect for bunking off, a route to take with someone precious. If we were stuck in the house it might be more difficult to feel so relaxed.

Without the comforting motion of the train, the passing scenery, I might not be able to let go of my current crop of worries – about how to make ends meet, the state of the roof on our house, which we need to sell so that we can move out of London, and finishing my first novel (I can't completely let go of that, and have a notebook on me in case inspiration strikes). The more I brooded on these matters, the more my daughter would sense my growing distraction, the atmosphere might become strained. But now everything is going just right. I know that something good will happen today.

We get off at Gospel Oak, on the edge of Hampstead Heath. A friend recommended the playground here, a few minutes walk from the station. It's much nicer than the grubby one full of broken equipment surrounded by loping, hooded teenagers in the middle of Walthamstow. It's packed and noisy, my daughter tightly clutches my hand, nervously eyes the yelling throng on the climbing frame, the whirling mob on the roundabout. She's uneasy in this unfamiliar territory, a long way from home. It's hard work persuading her that it's worth the effort to join the queue and wait patiently for a go on the swings. The magic of the train ride soon dissipates. After a couple of minutes she starts complaining.

'Daddy, I'm bored.'

It *is* tedious, waiting for our turn. Far easier to do something else instead, then come back later. But if we move on now, I know she will abandon the idea of having a turn on the swings, and I don't want this to happen. She *loves* going on the swing, and I enjoy watching her delight as she flies through the air.

'Faster! Faster!'

Plus these swings *work*.

There's something else too.

I don't want her to get into the habit of giving up too easily, something it seems to me that I did much too often when I was young. My Catholic upbringing reinforced ad nauseam the idea that not getting what you want is a virtue, till I wanted to explode with frustration as I watched others have all the fun. That, at least, is how it seems in retrospect. This mustn't happen to my daughter. So I insist that we stay where we are, no matter how much she complains.

But there's a boy next to us in the queue who's really getting on my nerves. I cannot identify who is in charge of him. He's probably no more than six, but he's a lot larger, much more confident than my daughter. He started off waiting behind us, but has edged slowly but surely forward, so that he is now standing right next to her. Another boy greets him and he replies in an offhand way in a plummy voice, barely glancing his way. He is totally and utterly focused on the swings, scanning them like a hunter, poised for take-off the moment one is free. He stands straight-backed, hands on hips, chin jutting out, looking for all the world like a junior version of a British army officer. A typically confident and assertive NW3 child, I think. There isn't a speck of dirt on his immaculate green polo shirt or pristine white shorts, nor a hair out of place on his expensively groomed head. He seems to have rushed here straight from doing a photo shoot for the latest *Next* catalogue. The parents around me are swapping gossip about high-powered jobs, rising house prices, prospective schools. Their children are the opinion formers, the movers and shakers, the internet entrepreneurs of the future.

He steps on my daughter's foot, doesn't even notice her flinching.

'Hey! Watch what you're doing.'

He catches my expression, startled. Mutters something, quickly looks away. My daughter begins pulling at my hand, muttering '*Daddy*' in an accusing tone. This is now beginning to feel like a punishment to her – why can't we leave it? But by now we are at the head of the queue.

'It won't be long now sweetheart, we're next.'

The boy is like an Olympic sprinter poised on the starting line. I just *know* that he is going to run and grab the next vacated swing before us. I feel the anger building inside me – how dare this pushy little Hampstead brat try and edge in front of my shy, well behaved little girl. I picture a future where she is repeatedly edged out of the way by people like him. Oh yes, I have his number all right. His parents probably moved house just so they could get him into the right primary school – gazumping someone else at the last minute. They have a holiday home in the south of France, pushing up house prices there too, forcing out poor peasants. They clog up the streets with their ghastly four-wheel drive and have a Filipino maid who they beat savagely and force to sleep in a broom cupboard. He has a bedroom stuffed full of expensive toys and games. A private tutor. Stocks and shares in his name. He will inherit a fortune and think it is his just dessert and that poor people have only themselves to blame for their plight. He has all the things that we cannot afford to give our daughter but oh no, that's not enough – *on top of all that he wants her swing as well!*

Over my dead body.

My jaw tightens. My back straightens. I take a step forward, practically dragging my daughter with me. I know that I am being ridiculous, but I don't care.

'*Daddy!*'

She is trying to tug me back. She senses the machismo rising, and doesn't like it. This wasn't what she had in mind when I told her about the nice playground we were going to visit. I turn around to reassure her that everything is going to be alright, that we'll have that swing any moment now. She's staring beyond me, her face falling. I turn back and see the boy running to a just vacated swing.

The little so-and-so has pushed in.

I'm not having it.

I let go of her hand and stride over to where he's steadying the still moving seat.

'Excuse me.'

He looks up, shocked. No longer the junior officer, but the little boy that he actually is. For a moment I feel sorry for

78

him. How intimidating, to be confronted with this towering, scowling adult. I push this feeling swiftly to the back of my mind.

'You jumped the queue. My daughter was next, she's been waiting for a long time.'

I feel obliged to cloak my anger with what I hope is an air of reasonableness. Clearly, if we dispense with orderly queuing and allow the democratic order to break down, we'll descend into total anarchy and end up having to call in the SAS to patrol our playgrounds. No, this kind of behaviour must be nipped in the bud. Yes, that's the kind of tone I'm trying to project. However there's a secret part of me that desperately wishes I could act like my father would have done in this situation. His inability to control his ferocious temper, his ignorance of what constituted acceptable social behaviour seems, right now, heroic and liberating. How I would love to explode like him. To subject this boy to the kind of blistering display of anger that he regularly subjected me to as a boy.

Feck off out of it ya little whelp ya, that's my daughter's swing. If you don't give it to her right now, I'll give ya a bleddy clout round the gob!

But I am highly educated, the first member of my family to go to university, I read the *Guardian* and *Observer*, go to art house cinemas to watch subtitled films by Polish directors and discuss their finer points afterwards. I am a published writer. I am not a poor, downtrodden Irish migrant. I was born here, I know how this society works, I know it's codes and assumptions from the inside. I will hate myself if I let go like that and terrify this boy. So, instead, and this feels a very poor second best, I simply stand there and give him a cool look to let him know that I mean business. I even say 'Thank you' without too much sarcasm when he reluctantly gets off the swing.

I turn around and beckon my daughter forwards, a triumphant smile on my face.

'Come on sweetheart.'

She frowns, shakes her head. Her face is a picture of misery.

I don't believe this.

'*Come on.*'

She stays where she is. I've made too big a deal of it. She's desperately uncomfortable, too aware of the people watching all this. I know, straight away, that there's no way I'm going to get her on that swing now. She turns her face away, hunches her shoulders. I walk across, take her hand and lead her to another part of the playground.

You don't have to queue for the sandpit, so that's where we go next. I play with her there for a long time, trying to put the whole swing incident behind us. We have a go on the seesaw afterwards, then the roundabout (I am the only adult there, and end up pushing seven or eight kids round and round) and then stand next to her as she goes on to try out the climbing frame. It's the sandpit that has caught her imagination today though, and she wants to play there again.

There is another girl there about her own age (her mother sits on a bench nearby, talking on her mobile) and eventually they begin playing together. Though to be more accurate, what they really do is play side by side, without really interacting, in the way that children of that age do. Satisfied that she is fully engaged, relaxed and happy, that she is experiencing *flow*, I begin stepping slowly back. I have not left her side for a moment since we've been here, and I think it's time that she did something without me hovering. I am going to join the other girl's mother on the bench and soak up the sun, take out my book and read one of Frank O'Connor's wonderful short stories. I take a few steps towards the bench, stop, check on her, carry on, stop and check, carry on.

Then, in the middle of playing, she suddenly turns around to check where I am. When she doesn't see me, the sheer panic on her face is instant and intense. I find it almost unbearable to watch. It's a struggle to force down the impulse to call out her name. For that would only signal that if I am out of her sight for only a moment it is a big deal. We have discussed the need to foster her independence, her mother and I. We have agreed that if every time she experiences some kind of uncertainty or distress we instantly rush to reassure her it will only serve to reinforce her dependence on us, end up limiting her freedom. So I stand where I am, not moving, not speaking, doing nothing whatsoever to attract attention to myself. I have the perfect view of my daughter's distress. She's nervously scanning the unfamiliar adults scattered around. There is a burning in my chest, my throat constricts. I will her to notice me, put an end to this agonising moment.

Come on, turn a bit more this way. I'm right here.

I am ready. I am waiting. Standing there, doing nothing, saying nothing, *letting go*, is one of the hardest things I've ever done. I had no idea that doing nothing could be so excruciating. Every muscle, every nerve, is straining to *do* something. The adrenalin starts pumping through me. With it comes another upsurge of machismo – I would leap into a burning house to save her, charge a man with a gun holding her hostage. But she isn't trapped in a burning house, or being held hostage. She is standing ten feet away from me in a playground on a lovely summer's day surrounded by middle class *Guardian* readers on the border with Hampstead.

Then she adjusts her position again, and sees me. I smile as if nothing has happened. As if my heart hasn't turned over and my guts haven't twisted into a knot. I hold up my hand and wave, and watch her fear disappear. The relief and happiness on her face is the perfect reward, and I feel like I'll never have to justify my existence again. Reassured, she returns to her game. And I stay where I am, utterly distraught. I know that this is a positive thing. That a small lesson has been learnt. That she's taken a minor step towards greater independence. Something good has happened here today. It just doesn't feel like it.

This one, brief, seemingly insignificant episode is burnt into my mind, has greater resonance than many other occasions that seemed much more worrying at the time. Like the day I left the room to answer the phone and came back to find that she'd fallen down the steep concrete steps to the garden and cut her lip open. Or the Sunday afternoon we rushed her to casualty with a soaring temperature, fearing meningitis. Maybe it's because this episode crystallizes the difficult balancing act all parents have to strive for. Providing enough love and support to enable their child to feel confident and happy, yet keep enough distance so that you don't smother them.

Your children are not yours forever, you only have them on loan.

***

It's three years later. We are living in Leeds now, my daughter is in her second year at school. I am reading her a bedtime story, *The Enchanted Horse*, about a rocking horse who comes to life and takes her owner, a little girl, on magical journeys. She loves anything to do with horses at the moment. Earlier we had played her favourite game, the one where I get down on all fours and pretend to be her horse. She rides around the room on my back, giggling and scolding me when I'm not obedient, rewarding me with (imaginary) sugar lumps when I've been good.

I finish the chapter, put out the light, say goodnight. As I'm leaving the room she shouts 'No, don't go. I don't want you to leave.'

Her voice, so small and vulnerable in the dark, cuts deep into me. I ask her what's wrong.

'I'm sad.'

It's been a long, hard day, I'm tired and hungry, and the delicious smell of a takeaway from Raja's is wafting up the stairs – onion bhajis, malai kofta, garlic and coriander nan are waiting below. But there's something in her tone that convinces me this is more than a standard delaying tactic. Plus I'm feeling guilty – for weeks now I've been too busy, too harassed, too preoccupied, to give her the amount of time and attention that a six-year-old needs and deserves.

'Why are you sad?'

'I want you to always be my dad.'

I'm caught off guard – I didn't expect that.

'Of course I will.'

My tone is calm and reassuring, but I'm thinking *oh no, are we going to have to talk about me dying now?* They say there's nothing like becoming a parent to put you in touch with your own mortality.

She says, 'No you won't,' close to tears now. Alarmed, I walk over to her bed, crouch down, gently place my hand on her shoulder.

'I'll always be your dad, no matter what.'

But she won't have it. Something has upset her, and she repeats again and again that *I won't*, shaking her head from side to side. I feel an iron band tightening around my chest. How could she doubt my love? With my other hand I begin gently stroking her cheek.

'Even when you're grown up,' I tell her in a soothing voice, 'Even after you've left home and are living somewhere else – even if you decide to have children of your own and become a mother, I'll *still* be your dad.'

But none of this cuts any ice with her. She shakes her head.

'No, no you won't.'

The tears are welling up in her eyes and she kicks off the covers. She's angry – that she can't find the right words to make me understand; that I can't grasp what's upsetting her so much and am forcing her to try and spell it out.

'*Why* won't I be your dad when you grow up?'

She begins to cry.

'Because you'll just be a man.'

This stuns me into momentary silence. My six-year-old daughter has had the kind of insight about her relationship with her father that many people don't achieve until they reach their thirties. Over the next few days, I find myself wondering what conclusions my daughter will reach when she does eventually come to see me as just a man? The thought of her future verdict makes me uncomfortable. How long, I wonder, before she is ready to conduct that enquiry into who she is and how she came to be that person? Ten years? Twenty? Thirty? However long it is, I hope that I'm still around, so she doesn't have to manage it without one of the key witnesses she'll need to interrogate.

Why did you do that?

You should have told me earlier.

You may have thought you were doing the right thing, but it wasn't –

not for me, at any rate.

Hopefully I'll be compos mentis and capable of having the kind of conversation with her that might be of some help. The type of conversation I would love to have had with my own father – to have asked him how he felt about being my dad, and told him what it was like for me being his son.

I remember how painful the process of coming to see *my* father as just a man was. A process that he was unable to help me with, being patently unable to help himself, instead covering up his fear and confusion with ranting and raving guaranteed to push everyone away. He wasn't the kind of man who took kindly to being asked questions.

How should I know?

Ask your mother.

Can't you see I'm busy?

I'm pleased that my daughter is able to ask me things, even when her questions make me uncomfortable. Delighted that my relationship with her will be very different to the one that I had with my father. Though sometimes, when I'm tired and irritable and she asks me something awkward that I don't want to deal with, a little bit of me envies the kind of behaviour that my dad could get away with. Then I, too, want to yell and roar.

How should I know?

Ask your mother.

Can't you see I'm busy?

But I don't. Because I am still a father. It will be some

years yet before I become just a man again. I must make the most of the time available to me.

We are discussing autobiography at the creative writing class I teach at Leeds University. At the end of the session I talk about *Four Fathers*. I tell them about the conversation with my daughter that I have just described, and what I think it means. And Sylvia says, *Actually Ray, your interpretation of your daughter's remark is quite wrong. You can never be just a man ever again. No matter what happens, you'll always be a father now, there's no going back*. She says this quietly, but with great assurance, and smiles. As well she might. I realize, instantly, that she is absolutely right. Just as I will shape and change my daughter's life irrevocably, so she has irrevocably shaped and changed mine.

I am taking my daughter to school on a cold, January morning. In the last year I have watched her grow more confident, more gregarious. Now, in the morning, she does not want me to hold her hand once we reach the school. Kissing goodbye is out of bounds too. While I am bending down to tie our crazy dog to the railings a friend of hers calls out my daughter's name, then charges up and throws her arm around her. They waltz into school together, a couple of tearaways, giggling at some joke that is not meant for me, while I ensure that the dog is on a short enough lead to prevent her from leaping at passers-by. Then I follow them through the school gates and into the milling throng.

Before I was a father, when I was just a man, to see

someone I loved prefer someone else's company to mine would have been a hammer blow. What did I know back then? No matter, for I can never be just a man again, not any more. Now I will always be a father, and though fatherhood hasn't given me any answers, and all the doubts, anxieties and questions that plagued me when I was a man remain, indeed, have multiplied, at least I have discovered another source of joy and hope that wasn't there before. She is finding her own way now, is already beginning to leave me behind. What more could a father ask?

Inheritance

John Siddique

I

For the last few days I have been scouring the net trying to find an address for the UK office of *The Daily Jang*, the biggest newspaper in Pakistan.

I believe my father is still alive. I have had no news of him since 1992 and did not know where he was living even then. Being in my forties, 1992 doesn't seem very long ago, so I count it on my fingers, and the distance opens up even further. All I know about Dad's last whereabouts is from when he took us in 1970 to Pakistan to meet the Indian side of the family. They had survived the forced march across the border from India when my father was a boy of fifteen, and settled in a region of The Pakistani Punjab called Rahim Yar Khan.

Shouldn't you be able to feel if your father is dead?

Finding the name of Rahim Yar Khan has been a task that has taken me a long time. My mother is still reticent to speak about the journey and our time in Pakistan. I have managed to coax stories from her over the last decade, in the form of little descriptions of places we passed through – but she has not been able to remember the name of where we went. Whether her forgetfulness is by choice I don't know.

Over the last few years I have asked anyone who I thought might know of this vague place. 'My mum has told me it was Rrmmmsomething, I can't bloody remember.' I would often find myself stumbling, embarrassed. Sitting quietly amongst the administrative bustle in the gallery offices at Cartwright Hall one lunchtime, I got talking to a woman called Robina. Her son attends a school I had done some poetry days at. He had written a lovely poem about her.

I asked her. 'How well do you know Pakistan?'

'Quite well, we go over every year to visit our parents.'

I wondered if she could help me find the place where we stayed. I told her about my childhood visit, that I knew that we had been somewhere in the north. I told her about the brightness of the sun. How people danced in the rain. The taste of the sugar cane in my mouth. I described the smell of bread coming from the clay ovens built into the ground. And how I was always running between the cotton rows and past the cows – who stared warily at me – to my uncle's tenement farm. Before the rains we had stayed in a big town for a while. It was all white buildings. Our house had a veranda and there was always a busy hubbub outside. I said my parents had gone their separate ways not long after these adventures, that I wished I knew more about my father. She told me she didn't know the places I talked about, but that her husband might. She rang him there and then.

When she got off the phone, she told me that there was a

place called Rahim Yar Khan. Her husband was going to ring his brother in Pakistan to see if my vague description and the place might match up. The next day she told me that her brother-in-law rang back and that it sounded like the right place. When I came back after lunch she had gone home but had left me a note saying that her brother-in-law would help me if I ever went to Pakistan and needed some help.

That was a year ago.

Now I find myself picking up the phone to begin the process, it's like hauling a great weight inside. I was six when we came to the end of our journey, it was also when my father stopped living with us properly. My mother and sisters and I left him at Karachi airport when we returned to the UK in 1971. After we returned home he would turn up for a week or so, once a year, round about Christmas or New Year. He kept turning up until I was thirteen and then his visits stopped. That is until a broken-down version of the once giant man arrived in Manchester for three days in 1992. He was small. He walked miles around the city as he couldn't figure out the buses. And he just kept saying – pleading rather – that he wanted to get us all back as a family again. Back then the quest of wanting to get to know him had not yet begun for me. Now I kick myself for not taking proper advantage of what is probably the last time I would see him. I was so full of my mother's stories about him, I let him come and go without getting to know him any better.

Today I called the paper, placed the advert and began to wait.

> *I am trying to find my father Mohammed Siddique, I have not seen him for many years, I would like just to know him again. I believe he was last living in the Rahim Yar Khan region, he was born 1/10/1931. He lived in Rochdale, England in the 1960s and was married to Norah O'Neill. He has four children by her; John, Kathleen, Ann, and Jacqueline. He was living in Pakistan in 1992 and had remarried. If you know anything of him or his whereabouts, please write to me.*

> *Thank you*

> *John Siddique*

There is so much to tell him. Will I have to be the one to tell my father that his youngest daughter died of cancer at the age of twenty-five? His little visits gave us Jacqueline, and she didn't stay around too long. If I find him he will now be an old man, I will never have known him in his full manhood. The part of me that is still five years old remembers him as a grumpy big faced giant chasing me around. The twenty-eight-year-old remembers him shrunken and depleted. How small will he be if I ever get to see him? His smoothness will have gone, that dapper suit-wearing man proud and white-shirted, reduced in both bone and skin. If and when we meet, will it be me who is the adult, and he who is like the son? I don't know what I'll say to him. These are the sorts of things I practice but they're never right when I get there, or rather they're the sort of things that slip away whenever I try to bring them into clarity.

II

The world throws impossible coincidences at us sometimes. Today is one of those days for me. The advert to try and find my dad is in the paper. I don't know if I'll get anything from this first casting-out, but I'm hoping that the ripples that flow out from this intention will touch someone out there. This process needs a huge set of coincidences to occur. I'm waiting for an unknown person in a unknown country to see the paper. For them to read the ad amongst all the news and the classifieds, then for a memory to stir in that person. For that recognition to be enough for them to do something, and for the outcomes of this viral networking to then flow back in my direction.

I feel like I'm asking a lot of the universe, and yet I expect an answer.

On the same day that these wheels begin turning, a letter arrives from my ex's son, Simon. Family is a difficult thing. It refuses to be the shapes defined in popular culture. It is far from being simple or straightforward. It has nothing to do with blood – and everything to do with blood. When there is blood between you it is always there to fall back on, no matter where things go. Blood is a fact, undeniable, genetic and concrete.

I believe that soul is just as solid as blood. The law likes blood. It makes things easier. Soul complicates matters. There is no proof except the spirit's own movement. Simon is part of my family, as is his sister Rose, and their mother. I have not seen Simon to speak to for over two years since my relationship with his mother fell apart. When relationships end, if you are not married so much more gets lost than just the other person. In this case I lost a partner, two kids, and an extended family that I belonged to as if they were my own. This experience is not unique. This kind of loss is common, everyday. Ordinary, even. But they are not my kids, not my blood, my genes – and there is no paper to prove anything. We live with it. And the people around us lose the ability to hear what we're trying to say. They reply 'Oh dear' and shrug their shoulders.

I have spotted Simon three times in the last two years. The first two times we just looked broken-heartedly at each other and did not speak. The second time I walked back to where I'd seen him after passing but he was gone. The third time I was driving and could not stop, but we smiled at each other. He has left school now. I could see from our brief exchange that he is becoming his own person. I decided to send him a card to say how good it was to have eye contact, how lovely it was to see him and that I hoped he was doing well.

Today, of all the days, when my yearnings for family are dancing tentative new shapes, he writes;

Hi John

Thanks for your card. That was really nice to hear from you. I was glad I saw you that day, and we noticed each other. Normally one of us is not noticed. I hope your book goes well, and hope you're okay and feeling happy. I am at the moment. My job's going really well, I love what I do. It's great. I am doing a joinery apprenticeship and going to college doing woodwork occupations (carpentry).

I've finally got some technics as well (1200s, the silver ones) they're brilliant, and I've got a load of good vinyl as well. Sorry about my writing. It's not very good as you can see.

Mum mentioned you might be leaving town. If you do, make sure you stay in touch. I'm downstairs now, on my own. The doorway between what was the kitchen and the old dining room, which is now my bedroom, has finally been blocked up. It's nice. It's like having my own place.

Hope everything is going well for you as it is for me. My budgie died but someone gave me a cockatiel not long ago. He's called Billy. Anyway I'll go now, as I'm just about to get in bed. Write back soon.

Lots of love, Simon xxx

P.S. I didn't forget you, you know. You helped me a lot and gave me good advice and were a good 'mum's boyfriend'.

Always thinking of you

x

People – friends – tell me all sorts of odd things about time. When I try to talk to them about this stuff, they say that 'time is a great healer'. Or that 'you shouldn't waste time on these things and just get on with your life'.

Strangers sometimes tell you better varieties of truth.

It's funny how conversations can happen on trains, or in a pub somewhere, on remote coastal paths, and in airport lounges. There's time to kill and nothing to lose, and I know I'll never see them again, so it's easier to tell the truth.

There is an accumulated truth I have learned from these meetings – these temporary friendships – and occasional encounters with genuine angels: that time heals nothing. New love doesn't fix old things, family is never forgotten, and it doesn't go away. All time does is put layers of life in between you and whoever or whatever it is. We learn perspective, distance, how to do things in new ways and how to place the ornaments we make of life in a kind of display case in our hearts. Perhaps to create a menagerie from them, or a set of memories that suit our needs and love.

Something else I have found from these conversations is that people start collecting things to fill the shapes they've been left with: toy soldiers, classic sci-fi DVDs, things for their car, money, watches, art, electronic solutions to aid everyday living. Some people drink. Some people drug. And some throw themselves over and again at love. That's how we do it, and heaven love us for our ways.

Just by living we gather family. It's the natural function of life. All we can do is love them the best we can. And if we're lucky, brave or daft enough we can keep them in our lives as we try to understand what blood means, what soul means, and what family means.

For me they are ripples on the lake of my father.

Each glimpse of Simon, each letter, each conversation with any news of them is a stone thrown into water. I can't see my dad because he stands behind me. To my left and right blood family and soul family. We walk to the water, everyone who has belonged in my life has drunk there, and watched the ripples from the skimmed stones spread out and bounce back in inference.

In loco parentis

James Nash

It is late on Friday afternoon. The classroom is quiet and extremely hot. Outside, through a subtropical heat, Meanwood dozes like a dog on a warm pavement. I am sweating slightly. The crucifix above the blackboard glints bronze on black wood. This is my most difficult class; a ragamuffin crew of twenty noisy, feral children who test every nerve and sinew, every reserve, every jot of understanding. Knowing that I will be teaching them for another three years – no-one else wants to and I am the Head of Department – I feel impaled on them and by them.

It is 1974 and I am just twenty-five. Having completed an MA in English Literature, I intended to be an academic, but after an arduous vacation job working as a supervisor in a boys' remand home, I trained as a teacher. I am still surprised to find myself in a classroom, still find my affinity for 'naughty' or 'thick' children unexpected. Others are surprised too. Only this week another member of staff suggests that I am teaching these 'remedial' children and therefore presumably not the children of the moneyed, professional classes for political reasons; apparently my plummy tones and long-haired good manners are so at odds with the kind of kids I teach that I have to have some underlying agenda.

I look at my class. We have just finished measuring our heights with a tape lent to us by the needlework teacher. We also have weighed ourselves on scales 'borrowed' by Sean from the medical room. The bathroom set I had brought from home creaked and gave up the ghost under the weight of the third hulking adolescent to bounce onto them. It was a hilarious and potentially risky half-hour at the front of the classroom, where I stood like a circus ringmaster and the pupils twirled about me in a more or less disciplined way. Now they are settled in comparative quiet, translating their findings onto graph paper. I watch each child warily. It is Friday afternoon, when everybody including myself is on a short fuse.

I look over at Sean. I realise I look at him a lot. I have the anxiety of a mother with a premature baby where Sean is concerned, as if, in his obvious failure to thrive, he might one day just slip away from me, a teenage cot death. Someone has broken him. His hands are filthy with an ingrained dirt that makes his skin shine like old leather. His mother, a frizzy blonde with penciled-in eyebrows, is an alcoholic. She was probably drinking throughout her pregnancy with Sean, who in consequence is not wired up properly. His blue eyes are often unfocussed. He likes me sitting next to him in class, when I help him with his work, and sometimes moves so close to me that I can often feel his breath on my cheek or arm.

But he also sings Elvis songs very loudly and on a continuous loop. Today's number is *Return to Sender*. When he reaches the climax of the song, he tips himself backwards over in his chair and crashes to the floor to the cheers of his classmates. Everything comes to a laughing standstill and I hear from myself the measured, patient voice I use to deal with this five-times-a-lesson behaviour.

'That's OK Sean. Just get up now. And remember that you could easily hurt yourself doing that.'

These light remonstrations always calm him for about seven minutes. And then the singing starts again, quiet at the beginning, slowly building to a crescendo. He is peaceful at the moment, feels my gaze on him, and catching my eye, grins at me. His obvious affection humbles and embarrasses me.

The boy next to Sean is Ryan, blue-eyed and black-haired. He is colouring in his bar chart with felt-tip pens, his tongue slightly protruding from his fleshy mouth in concentration. He was small last year. But aged thirteen he suddenly began to bulge out of his clothes in a daunting, hormonal way. Now he has started patting the girls' bodies as they pass his desk in the classroom. For some of the quieter girls this is torture, for others his dangerous, edgy personality is a complete turn-on. He can flip into an incandescent rage within seconds, and on these occasions is a danger to himself and others. One day, I am sure, he will kill somebody. It might be himself, or more likely a complete stranger who looks at him sideways in a pub. I see how he is wracked by demons. Perhaps he has seen too much, or too much has happened to him. Much of what he is at fourteen is sexual, the bullying, the seething excitement, and the way he rolls his sleeves high above his adolescent biceps. Fifteen years later, on a visit, I will see him sitting on his own in a prison recreation area.

The lanky girl is called Philomena. She plays football with the lads in the yard at break-time when most boys baulk at tackling her. She is too fierce and fearless for them. She has a strong jaw-line and angry blue eyes that say, quite clearly, 'Get off me!' Her handwriting is large, open and extraordinarily neat. In a classroom where personal hygiene is not a top priority, or perhaps even a possibility, her cleanliness is unusual. Philomena was once criticised by her female PE teacher for trying too hard to win in a netball match. Her response, 'Fuck off, you stupid bitch,' was not well received by the teacher concerned.

The rest of the class is somnolent in the heat. A mass of dark, fair and red hair bent over their books. Sometimes I love all of them. Sometimes we all laugh together about something that one of them says. Once Carmel, a large scruffy girl with long arms and legs and an engaging smile, says in her pretty, unreconstructed Irish accent, 'You're very tall for a teacher, Mr Nash.' And for some reason that sets us all off. A similar thing happened on the day I wore a dark green shirt and trousers. I realised from the stifled giggles that something was going on, but only worked out by lunch-time that every child had set themselves the task of using the word 'green' at some point in the morning.

In the middle of the classroom Doyle puts his hand up. Quiet and stolid he is mostly unnoticed. But nobody messes with him. He will have made a mistake with his work, or thinks he has, putting children on his bar chart in the wrong order, drawing his grid upside down, or spelling the names all wrong. I reassure him that what he is doing is fine and move over to the blackboard where I chalk up the title for today's maths, The Heights and Weights of Our Class. I always think I fail an essential test of being a real teacher when I write on the board. My writing loops untidily in a downward, unprofessional slope. In the background I hear Sean begin to rev up.

'Return to sender, address unknown, no such number, no such…' I sometimes find myself humming his songs on the days I cycle home. I sigh a little, feeling myself stretched a touch too far. One of the timid, mouse-like girls puts her hand up.

'Please, Sir, can I borrow a pencil, Sir?'

'Yes, Joan,' I say, and hold up the box from my desk. She has been blessed with the unlikely name of Joan Crawford, but has none of her film namesake's personality. She is no Mildred Pierce, so looking at the space between herself and me, she works out where Ryan is in relation to her journey across the classroom; she is one of the girls for whom Ryan's patting and touching is unbearable.

Sean is reaching the main chorus of his song just as Joan is passing behind him. He makes a quick decision not to fling himself back in his chair, catches my eye and grins. I grin back. We both know that he has been stymied of his grand finale, because Sean would not actually hurt anyone. He likes getting hurt and going off to the medical room with cuts or bruises to be tended to by the school secretary, a kind and attractive woman in her forties who always smells of *Je Reviens* scent, and can wind him round her little finger.

Ryan moves out of his desk and comes towards me. He has broken his pencil. I just saw him press the point down on his page, deliberately hard to break it. I tense slightly, as I always do when Ryan does something. Somehow he manages to reach the front of the classroom just after Joan. I hand her a pencil and she turns and walks into Ryan. His hand reaches up in front of her and he cups her breast in his hand. He squeezes it. She looks towards me, and her eyes brim with tears. I suddenly feel a hot rage welling up inside me. I loathe Ryan's sexual bullying, and I hear a roar coming from inside my chest, and it is my father shouting.

'Ryan, don't do that, you disgusting little sod.'

The class collectively gasps at my swearing, and everyone looks over to our frozen tableau at the front of the classroom. Sean has put his hands over his ears, and for once is avoiding meeting my eye. He hates me shouting. I sometimes wonder if it reminds him of his absent and violent father. Joan is bright red. Ryan has bunched his fists as if ready to fight off censure or criticism, and I have moved forward to put myself between Joan and Ryan. Ryan looks totally exposed with the attention of the whole class on him, and I see a strange light in his eye. I push myself between them and Ryan pretends that I have hurt him. His eyes fill with tears. They look like thick lenses. He sees his fellow classmates, and snarls at them.

'What do you think you're staring at?'

Philomena laughs once. It sounds like the coughing of a large dog. She has never been touched by Ryan. He has a healthy respect for her since she elbowed him on one of the rare occasions he played football. Ryan does not put himself into situations where he may look foolish or which expose cracks in his frail machismo. After this confrontation with Philomena he has not played football again.

His eyes burn in his face. And suddenly he is running. Running towards the window at full tilt. It is clear what he is going to do. The boy who once threw himself in front of a school bus, because he was told to queue in an orderly fashion, is going to jump through the open window. We are three floors up. Sean is humming loudly and very fast, and for once it is completely unconscious, a soundtrack rather than a way of muffling and blanking out the world. Ryan hooks one leg over the window sill, and slides the window open more widely by simply jamming his body through it. I am there one second after him, and grab at the arm and leg which are still in the classroom.

The class is quiet, sitting like Easter Island statues, with frozen expressions. Ryan is crying now. Big, shaking sobs, but still he pushes on through the window. Suddenly in the corner of the classroom the tannoy crackles, a bell chimes, and the voice of the head teacher can be heard. Slow and hesitant he says, 'As the chapel and hall are out of action for the next few days, let us end the afternoon with a prayer.'

It is enough to slow Ryan down, sufficiently divert his attention for me to gain the upper hand, and pull him back fully into the classroom. I find Doyle at my side. Big and muscular, a successful schoolboy boxer, he is imperturbable, grabbing Ryan's legs. Ryan is fully back in the classroom, and kicking at me just as the class come to the end of the Hail Mary, 'Pray for us sinners now and in the hour of our death.' Somehow I hang on to him until I can get him back in his chair. Doyle has an arm around his shoulders. All Ryan's violence and energy have gone. I can feel tenderness on my shins which will turn to bruises very soon. There are still ten minutes to go to the end of the day.

I know in a few minutes, his final duty of the day done, we will see the head walk across the car park, look around a little furtively, get in his car and disappear down the road and home. You could set your watch by it. The PE department see his car leaving and know that it is time to come off the school field and get their charges showered and changed.

Somehow I settle the class down again. It is Friday 'sweetie time', where I talk to them about what has gone well in the week, who has excelled in different areas of behaviour or achievement, and hand out chocolates to those whose names I mention. I get a box of Quality Street out of my stock room. The children are silent in anticipation. Sean has stopped humming, but is rocking a little, and looks at me anxiously, as if for reassurance. Doyle is still sitting next to

Ryan, with his arm loosely around the other boy's shoulder. His father has a popular, if rough pub, in the centre of Leeds, and Doyle seems to have inherited, or learned, an ability to defuse situations, to recognise what might be needed in challenging circumstances. He seems to offer, by his very presence, a rocklike masculine reassurance which I envy. If only Doyle could spell and add up he could rule the world. Joan, now returned to her seat, is sill bright red with mortification at having her breast squeezed.

Philomena comes up for producing work of a high standard. Joan gets a mention for being helpful in handing out and collecting equipment and books at the beginnings and endings of lessons. Others come up for good English work, until finally I clear my throat in preparation for a potentially risky strategy, so that the class, and I, can leave on a high note for the weekend.

'And lastly two people who deserve special mention. Sean, not for keeping us entertained all week with *Return to Sender*, but actually for getting to lessons on time, and completing full attendance this week. Can't wait for next week's song, Sean.'

Sean is grinning widely from ear to ear as I continue.

'And last but not least Ryan whose behaviour was quite bad this afternoon, but in the event managed to pull himself round, and will perhaps now be able to give Joan an apology.'

Ryan mutters something in Joan's direction, who stares away from him, and the class get up and stand behind their chairs. I let them go a little early. Ten seconds can be the greatest gift a teacher can bestow on these kids, and I am left to contemplate the wreck of my classroom. I am exhausted by the trauma of the scene with Ryan, but also have the underlying exhaustion which each week as a teacher brings. I am still learning. I am still being tested in each lesson, and, against what can sometimes feel like insuperable odds, trying to be fair and consistent. I look round for the scales to find that Sean has already taken them back. Twenty minutes later I have tidied my room so that it is fit for the cleaners. As I pack my bag I am conscious of a pair of eyes on me. It is Sean waiting by the door. He is carrying a torn white plastic carrier bag from which a filthy football kit is issuing.

'Yes, Sean,' I say.

'Are you walking down to the bus, or are you on your bike, Sir?'

'I'm on the bus tonight, Sean. Are you walking down with me?'

And together we walk out of the school in a ritual that happens once every week or so. Much of our walk is in companionable silence until we reach the little parade of shops opposite the bus stop. A few people are going in and out of the newsagents for their evening paper. On this occasion Sean says, looking slightly away from me, 'Do you think people might think you're my dad, Sir?'

I look at him. He obviously hasn't done the maths. And as a teacher I am irretrievably middle-aged.

'They probably will,' I say.

And he grins at me. It is the right answer.

Author biographies

Ray French

Ray French was born in Wales to Irish parents. His first book was *The Red Jag and other stories* (Planet). His novel, *All This Is Mine*, is a Vintage paperback, and has been translated into Dutch and Italian. His second novel, *Going Under*, is to be published by Secker & Warburg. He is currently working on his third novel. He has taught Creative Writing for The Arvon Foundation and Leeds University and mentors other writers, as well as running fiction workshops. From autumn 2006 he is a Royal Literary Fund Fellow at Trinity & All Saints College, Leeds.

Visit his website at www.rayfrench.com.

James Nash

James Nash is Writer in Residence for Leeds University, Faculty of Education, and for High Schools in Calderdale. A long-time resident in Leeds, he is also a journalist, writing for *The Leeds Guide*, and editing the books page for the arts magazine *Northern Exposure.* Recently turning to prose, his third collection of poems, *Coma Songs*, was published in 2003.

Tom Palmer

Tom Palmer was born in Leeds. He is the author of five books: *The Bradford Wool Exchange* (1997), *If You're Proud to be a Leeds Fan* (2002), *Shaking Hands with Michael Rooney* (2006), *Football Writers' Handbook* (2006) and *More Readers Reading More* (2006). His stories have been published in collections published by Comma, Relish and Route. He has written for the *Observer*. He works in libraries promoting reading, often using sport as a way of exciting boys and men into loving books. He currently works freelance for the National Literacy Trust and The Reading Agency. He lives in Yorkshire with his wife and daughter.

John Siddique

John Siddique is both a father and a son, and has spent most of his life reflecting on the meanings of these roles. He is the author of *The Prize* (Rialto), and the editor of *Transparency* (Crocus Books). His work has appeared in numerous publications in the UK and abroad. His many commissions and residencies include Ilkley and Ledbury Festivals, The New Writing Partnership, HMYOI Wetherby, The Lowry, and BBC Manchester. He mentors and teaches creative writing both privately, and for institutions, including The Arvon Foundation and The Poetry Society. A well loved reader of poetry he travels internationally presenting his own work, and that of other writers he enjoys.

Visit his website at www.johnsiddique.co.uk

Acknowledgements

This book is dedicated to:

The Calderdale Assisted Conception Unit
Paddy French
Albert Morgan Nash, who enjoyed reading so much
Simon Howarth

The authors would like to express gratitude and thanks to the following people for their enthusiasm and support:

Melanie Abrahams, Clare Alexander, Diana Ashcroft, Ffion & Euan Atkinson, Craig Bradley, Rosemary Bullimore, Joolz Denby, Nadia Gilani, Sophie Hannah, Britta Heyworth, Rose, Simon & Chris Howarth, Ruth Jamieson, Jane Mathieson, Blake Morrison, Anne Mortimer, Bernard Murphy, Hannah Nunn, Rebecca Palmer, Louise Richards, Cheryl Roberts, Helen Robinson, Janet Scott, Jim Sells, Sarah Smythe, Janet Swan, Libby Tempest, Karen Thornton, Jack Thrisk, June Turner, Paula Truman, Su Walker, Peter Wallace, David Williamson and Pam Yates.

And thanks to the many others who have helped us – including the people who attended the *Four Fathers* events. We hope that you enjoyed listening to these stories about our fathers; we enjoyed hearing yours.

We would also like to say thank you to the following organisations and institutions for their support:

Bolton Libraries, Bradford Book Festival, Cheltenham Book Festival, Derbyshire Book Festival, Dexine, Eccles Library, Essex Book Festival, Halifax Libraries, Headingley Library, Leeds Libraries, Manchester Central Library, Off the Shelf Literature Festival, Oldham Book Festival, Route, Skipton Library, Spellow Library, HM Prison Sudbury, HM Prison Swansea, Trafford Libraries, Wakefield Libraries, Warrington Libraries, York Libraries.

Byteback books

Part One of *Four Fathers* was originally published as a byteback book.

The Three and a Half Day Parent

James K Walker

A young father is happy to be a split-parent. Half a week he looks after his son, the other half of the week he 'does drink'; a situation he advocates as a pragmatic way forward for the future of parenting. In this mini-collection of stories, a series of adult encounters with children in various scenarios have the cumulative affect of strengthening this case. *The Three and a Half Day Parent* is a funny and affectionate look at the relationship between adults and their children.

Happy Families

Editor: Oliver Mantell

Four stories about families by four distinctive and compelling storytellers: the love, the lies, the laughter, the loss. Happy Families features stories by Alexandra Fox, Penny Feeny, Chrissie Ward and Sean Burn.

Bitter Sky

Zdravka Evtimova

A sequence of short stories following the fortunes of Mona, the precious only daughter of Rayo the Blood. This is a warm and highly rewarding piece of storytelling from one of Bulgaria's leading writers. Bitter Sky reveals the nature of power and vanity in all its complexity and plays witness to the transformation of Bulgaria from a former part of the Eastern Block to part of the emerging new Europe.

Bloom

Editor: Emily Penn

Short and very short fiction exploring the realities of life in twenty first century Britain by the flower of our youth. Seven writers aged nineteen to thirty describe the now and the near future in this witty, enigmatic and engaging selection of stories.

Taking in the experience of first love, first jobs, urban desolation and a journey into the dark heart of rural Britain, this collection showcases a host of new writing talent well worth discovering.

Love of the Wild and Wayward

Mandy MacFarlane

What would you do if you discovered your betrothed to be spilling your secrets to his mates and laughing behind your back? Take another swig of chardonnay and blame it on the size of your knickers? Or string him up from the nearest tree?

Here, Mandy MacFarlane has produced a distinctive collection of fables and modern folk tales that get straight to the heart of relationship complexities and breezes through them with a power and clarity that comes only with this, the most original form of storytelling. It is true, there is a much more life affirming alternative to the current plague of chic lit, and this is it. Put away the chardonnay and pick up a full bodied red.

A full list of byteback titles and instructions on
how to make them up can be found at:
www.route-online.com

Route Books

Route Compendium

ISBN 1 901927 24 5

Price £8.99

Route Compendium is a festival of contemporary stories that brings together five of the first wave of Route's pioneering byteback books. Inside you will find five distinctive and original collections of contemporary fiction featuring: a showcase of bright young talent; the decorator's tale; stories of love and the trouble it can bring; modern folk tales and a collection of misfits which includes the most audacious car chase short story that you will probably ever read.

Wonderwall

ISBN 1 901927 24 5

Price £8.99

The Wonderwall is a spy hole into the world of other people. Meet Bradley, with his pointy shoes and his cloak; witness what transpires with Vernon, the pools-win baby; find out which coffee-shop serves the best scrambled eggs in Antarctica; see George measure his life in terms of how many biscuits he might eat; travel to the beach of the cocco-bella man.

A baker's dozen of wondrous stories that point a finger to the magic that exists within our day-to-day lives, and to the people who matter most, those close at hand.

Naked City

ISBN 1 901927 23 7

Price £8.95

At the heart of the modern city we find stories of lovers, stories of people with a desire to connect to someone else, something else. This collection reveals the experience of living through changing times, of people shaking the past and dreaming of better days, people finding their place, adapting to new surroundings, laughing and forgetting, living and loving in the grip of the city.

Included are a series of naked city portraits as seen through the lens of photographer Kevin Reynolds and a selection of the very best in new short fiction in a bonus section, *This Could Be Anywhere*.

Jack and Sal

Anthony Cropper

ISBN 1 901927 21 0

Price £8.95

Jack and Sal, two people drifting in and out of love. Jack searches for clues, for a pattern, for an explanation to life's events. Perhaps the answer is in evolution, in dopamine, in chaos theory, or maybe it can be found in the minutiae of domesticity where the majority of life's dramas unfold. Here, Anthony Cropper has produced a delicately detailed account of a troubled relationship, with a series of micro-stories and incidents that recount the intimate lies, loves and lives of Jack and Sal and their close friend Paula.

Kilo

M Y Alam

ISBN 1 901927 09 1

Price £6.95

Khalil Khan had a certain past and an equally certain future awaited until gangsters decided to turn his world upside down. They shattered his safe family life with baseball bats but that's just the beginning. They turned good, innocent and honest Khalil into someone else: Kilo, a much more unforgiving and determined piece of work. Kilo cuts his way through the underworld of Bradford street crime, but the closer he gets to the top of that game, the stronger the pull of his original values become.

Psychicbread

Mark Gwynne Jones

ISBN 1 901927 20 2

Price £6.95

Psychicbread introduces Mark Gwynne Jones and the space between our thoughts. Drawing on an ancient tradition, these captivating, mind altering poems tackle the complexities of our changing world with a beautiful humour. This collection presents the word in print, audio and film, coming complete with a CD of poems and stories.

Howl for Now

A celebration of Allen Ginsberg's epic protest poem

ISBN 1 901927 25 3

Price £9.99

In *Howl for Now*, academics, commentators and practitioners reflect on the power of 'Howl', half a century on from Ginsberg's historic first reading, through a series of essays and interviews.

Poet David Meltzer reflects on the San Francisco scene in the mid-1950s, Ginsberg collaborator Steven Taylor offers a personal memoir, film director Ronald Nameth and rock composer Bill Nelson contemplate a documentary version of 'Howl', and members of the University of Leeds consider the political, cultural and aesthetic place of the poem as both a social document and a point of contemporary inspiration.

For a full list of Route books
and for order details, please visit
www.route-online.com